SPYNOSAUR

NO MORE MR NICE

Where's Pugsy?!

SPYN

DEPARTMENT 6 ●○×≡

CLASSIFILE #14-06-MMXVIII

STRIPES PUBLISHING, an imprint of the Little Tiger Group
1 Coda Studios, 189 Munster Road, London SW6 6AW
A paperback original
First published in Great Britain in 2018

Text copyright © Guy Bass, 2018
Illustrations copyright © Lee Robinson, 2018

ISBN: 978-1-84715-909-0

A CIP catalogue record for this book is available
from the British Library.

Printed and bound in the UK.
10 9 8 7 6 5 4 3 2 1

DEPARTMENT
6

OSAUR

NO MORE MR NICE SPY!

GUY BASS ILLUSTRATED BY LEE ROBINSON

To Uncle Selwyn, still the funniest grown-up I've ever met
- Guy Bass

For Isaac, the only boy stronger than Spynosaur.
- Lee Robinson

Stripes

When top *spy*-entists put the mind of super-spy Agent Gambit inside the body of a dinosaur, they created the first ever **Super Secret Agent Dinosaur**. Together with his daughter, Amber, this prehistoric hero protects the world from villainy.

His code name:

SPYNOSAUR

FROM A LAND BEFORE TIME COMES A HERO FOR TODAY...

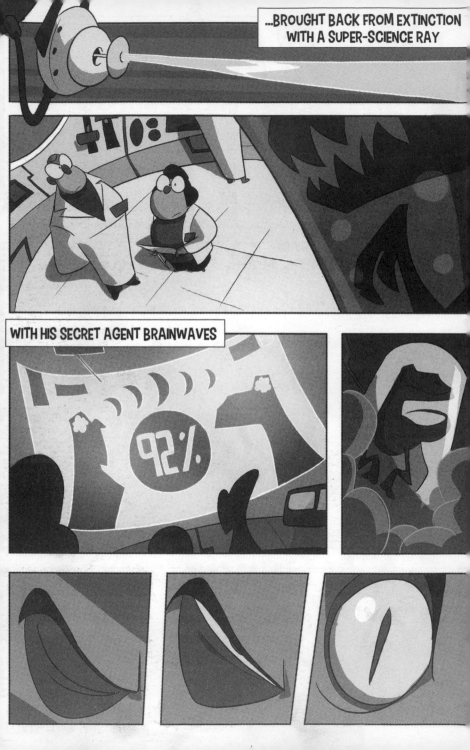

HE'S THE SCALED 'N' TAILED AGENT WHO IS CERTAIN TO SURPRISE

BUT HE STILL LOOKS LIKE A DINOSAUR, WHATEVER HIS DISGUISE

SPYNOSAUR!

1.
THE FATE OF ERGO EGO

⊙ ERGO EGO'S SECRET LAIR
THE BERMUDA TRIANGLE

"SPYNOSAUR!" screamed Ergo Ego. "You may have foiled my plans. But I will have revenge!"

DEPARTMENT 6 ●○✕≡

CLASSIFILE #1984-DZ-015

NAME:
ERGO EGO PHD.OMG.LOL.

>> Mind-bending villain.
Expert in illusion and mind
manipulation and creator of the
illusion-inducing "brain fog"
and Spynosaur's self-proclaimed
arch-enemy (SEE: SPYNOSAUR, DR
NEWFANGLE)

DEPARTMENT
6

Ego watched as Department 6 agents swarmed around his lair, dismantling his mind-control machines and going through his sock drawers.

"Revenge, I say!" the villain added. "R-E-V-V-E— No, wait, R-I-V-N…"

A shadow suddenly fell over Ergo Ego. He looked up to see Spynosaur looming over him. The scaly secret agent's lizard eyes glinted in the dim light of Ego's lair.

"Come to gloat, Spynosaur?" Ego hissed. "You may have thwarted me this time, but I'll be back! You'll never be rid of your arch-enemy!"

"Arch-enemy? Not sure I'd go that far," Spynosaur said, clamping Ego's wrists with hi-tech handcuffs. "I mean, I have a lot of enemies – Fandango Scaramoosh, Shady Lady, Gums Gambino..."

"Yes, but I'm the main one! I'm your *arch-enemy*, you stupid head!" Ego insisted. "I tied you to a space rocket and fired you into the moon, for goodness' sake! If it wasn't for me, you wouldn't be the dinosaur you are toda—!"

BA - DEEP!
BA - DEEP!

"Sorry, I need to get this," said Spynosaur, answering the call of his Super Secret Spy Watch™. "M11! Missing me already?" he said into the watch.

"What's that? A new criminal mastermind threatens world peace with his or her mad schemes? Sounds like a job for the world's greatest secret agent..."

With that, the scaly spy swept away and disappeared into the shadows.

"Wait, where are you going? Come back! Spynosaur! Don't ignore me, you stupid head!" screamed Ego as Department 6 agents led him away. "I'll prove I'm your arch-enemy! I'll make sure you never forget the name Ergo Ego! SPYNOSAUR!"

ONE YEAR LATER...

2.
ON THE RIGHT TRACKS

◈ ABOARD "THE SPEEDY BEAVER"
HIGH-SPEED LOCOMOTIVE,
ALBERTA, CANADA

"SPYNOSAUR!"

The cry rang out over Amber's Super Secret Spy Watch™. M11's voice was unmistakable – the head of Department 6 sounded like a foghorn being played through another foghorn.

●○✕≡

DEPARTMENT 6

CLASSIFILE   #1984-DZ-M11

CODE NAME: M11
(FORMERLY KNOWN AS A12)

>> Head of Department 6 and current wearer of the Moustache of Seniority. As hard as nails and tougher than overcooked steak. The only thing M11 loves are rules and her collection of antique moustache combs. In her spare time she enjoys going to work, avoiding holidays and shouting at Spynosaur.

DEPARTMENT
6

"Dad, it's M11!" Amber called out as she glanced down the train carriage. "She wants to know how the mission's going!" Amber added.

"Tell her we're on the right *tracks*," replied Spynosaur with a grin. The world's first and only secret agent dinosaur ploughed his way through a horde of hulking, black-clad thugs. The daring *deinonychus* punched, chomped and tail-swiped his way down the carriage, dispatching one brute after another with ferocity and flair.

"Blast it to smithereens, sidekick! Tell Spynosaur that time is running out!" M11 howled over Amber's watch. "Need I remind you both of the terrible fate that will befall the world should you fail?"

"I thought we were just rescuing some dumb dog," Amber replied.

"This is not just any dog! This is the princess of Canada's incredibly inbred priceless Peruvian pug, Pugsy Malone," M11 hissed. "The princess is on the warpath — if you fail to save her dog, she has vowed to unleash the full wrath of Canada upon the world! It'll mean all-out war!"

"Don't worry, M11 — we're just negotiating with the dog-nappers now," said Amber as a thug flew past her head and bounced along the corridor. She looked up and realized there was only one brute left standing. "Gottagocallyouback!" she said, ending her call with the press of a button. Then she vaulted over a seat and into the air. "SWIFTEST ARMADILLO HARDBACK EDITION RUBBER BAND ATTACK!"

With a flying, double-footed kick, she sent the last of the thugs crashing through a carriage window.

"Nicely done, Amber – I always said you were well *trained*," said Spynosaur with a grin.

"Da-ad, no puns," she groaned as they reached the door to the train's cab. "Well, we've been through all twelve carriages ... there's nowhere left to run."

"Indeed – ninety-nine knuckle-bruising pug-nappers down, one to go," Spynosaur concurred. He dug his clawed hands into the cab's door and it splintered and cracked like dried firewood. "Our pilfered pooch is behind this door, or I'm not the world's greatest secret—"

Spynosaur wrenched the door off its hinges and tossed it aside.

"—Huh," he added. The cab was empty.

What's more, the train controls were a smouldering wreck. *The Speedy Beaver* was hurtling along the tracks at full speed with no way to stop it.

"Ah, the old shift-the-train-on-to-an-unfinished-section-of-track-before-blasting-the-controls trick," said Spynosaur, glancing out of the window. "By my calculations we have precisely—" (Spynosaur pressed a timer on his Super Secret Spy Watch™) "—nineteen seconds before the train plummets off the end of the track into a bottomless ravine. That'll certainly *derail* our mission..."

Amber was about to deliver another groaning, "Da-ad," when:

YAP! YAP!

00:19

"The dog! But where...?" Amber said, her gaze drifting upwards. "Dad, the roof!"

Spynosaur helped Amber out of the cab window and they quickly clambered on to the roof of the speeding train. The slightest misstep would see them falling to a certain death. Amber couldn't have been happier with how the day was turning out.

00:11

Spynosaur peered down the length of the speeding train, squinting in the bright Canadian sunshine. A few metres away on the roof stood the hundredth hired thug, doing his best to stay upright as he tried to fire up a jetpack strapped to his back. Under his arm he carried a small, beige dog with a ridiculously squashed face and bulging eyes.

"Eww, *that's* the princess's precious pooch?" Amber said, screwing up her face. "What's wrong with it?"

"It's not Pugsy's fault he's a crime against nature," replied Spynosaur. He closed in on the thug, who was frantically pressing the jetpack's ignition switch. "Having a hard time getting your escape plan off the ground?"

00:08

"Don't come any closer, or I drop the dog!" the thug growled, dangling Pugsy over the edge of the train.

"I'd rather you didn't – the princess of Canada is one piece of bad news away from starting a war," replied Spynosaur. He winked at Amber. "You might say losing Pugsy would send her *over the edge...*"

"Over the edge..." Amber repeated, looking down the train tracks. Ahead, she could make out an iron barrier, signalling the end of the track. Beyond it, a vast ravine plummeting into nothingness.

"Dad, the tracks...!" she cried.

"Yes, I think this is our stop," her dad replied, checking his watch. "Grab Pugsy on the way down, will you?"

"On the way down?" Amber began. "What do you mea— AAAA!"

3.
HOW TO MAKE AN ENTRANCE

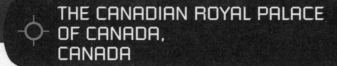

THE CANADIAN ROYAL PALACE
OF CANADA,
CANADA

"Where's Pugsy?" shrieked the princess of Canada.

The princess was barely a teenager, with a mass of frizzy black hair topped off with a sparkling tiara. She stamped around the throne room of the royal palace in a blindingly bejewelled dress. "Bring me back my Pugsy, or I'll blow it all up!"

The princess's servant scurried behind her, his bald, egg-shaped head beaded with nervous sweat.

"P-please try to stay calm, Your Majesty!" begged the servant, fretfully adjusting his oversized glasses and smoothing his long, white beard as he chased the princess around the room.

"I will not!" replied the princess with a rabid grunt. She spun round and eyeballed M11 at the other end of the throne room. The head of Department 6 had a neat bob of greying hair and an equally neat moustache, which twitched nervously as she hammered buttons on her Super Secret Spy Watch™.

"You!" snarled the princess, striding over to M11 with her servant hurrying behind. "Do something! You *promised* you'd rescue Pugsy..."

"I can assure Your Majesty I have my very best agent on the job," M11 replied. "If anyone can rescue Pugsy Malone, it's Spynosaur..."

"But if he messes up, you can still count on me!" came a cry. A monkey dressed in a spy-suit stepped into the princess's path.

DEPARTMENT 6

CLASSIFILE   #2-MALPA

CODE NAME:
DANGER MONKEY
AKA AGENT A41

>> Simian secret agent living in Spynosaur's shadow. Small, savage and second-best, Danger Monkey is always keen to prove his worth as a spy. Throws himself into every mission and usually ends up worse off as a result. Completely bananas.

DEPARTMEN

6

"The name's Danger Monkey — second-best agent in Department 6!" Danger Monkey declared, puffing out his chest. "Rest easy, Your Princessness — if Spynosaur messes up, I'll rescue your pig, or whatever it is. You can count on me to— **OOF!**"

With a swift kick, the princess booted Danger Monkey across the throne room. She rounded on M11. "Bring me Pugsy, or I blow it all up," she growled.

"Blast it to smithereens, Spynosaur!" M11 whispered, returning to her Super Secret Spy Watch™. "Where in the name of my moustache moisturiser are you?"

A low hum suddenly filled the air. M11 glanced up at the great, domed ceiling of the throne room. Through the perfectly polished glass she saw Spynosaur's jet-black spy-plane, the Dino-soarer, hovering in mid-air.

DEPARTMENT 6

CLASSIFILE   #1985-DZ-DB8

CODE NAME:
THE DINO-SOARER MKII

>> Supersonic saurian-styled stealth jet. Specially adapted for pilots with tails. Equipped with invisibility mode, gravity beam, missile launchers, front and rear laser cannons and built-in Wi-Fi.

DEPARTMENT 6

"Spyno!" cried Danger Monkey, scrambling to his feet as the Dino-soarer's docking bay swung open. Spynosaur and Amber leaped out from inside and crashed through the ceiling. As shards of glass cascaded through the air, the duo landed in the centre of the throne room and struck a stylish pose.

"*Smashing*," said Spynosaur.

"Spynosaur, you maddening maverick!" hissed M11. "This palace has doors, you know!"

"I prefer to *make* an entrance," he said. "And speaking of which..."

Spynosaur pointed a clawed finger skywards. Slowly descending through the air, suspended by the Dino-soarer's powerful gravity ray, was the princess of Canada's dog.

"Y-you see, Your Majesty? Pugsy is alive!" said the princess's servant, wiping his oversized brow in relief as Spynosaur plucked the pooch from inside the gravity ray and handed it to the princess.

"You saved him!" the princess cried as her dog snorted and wheezed. "You saved my Pugsy!"

"Actually, *I* saved Snotty McSmooshface from going splat," huffed Amber. "And I cleaned up the 'present' he left in the Dino-soarer..."

"Nice one, Spyno," said Danger Monkey, grudgingly. "I knew you'd save the day and leave no world savin' for the rest of us..."

"Indeed," added M11. "While it aggravates my stomach ulcer to congratulate you ... well done, Spynosaur. You may very well have prevented all-out war."

"Mr Spynosaur," added the princess's servant, sidling up to the saurian secret agent. He pushed his glasses up his nose with one hand and smoothed his beard with the other. "On behalf of the princess, Canada and world peace, thank you," he said, his egg-shaped head glistening. "May you get *everything* that is coming to you."

"All in half a day's work," replied Spynosaur. For a moment, he thought the servant looked oddly familiar ... then the princess rushed into Spynosaur's arms to give him a grateful hug, squashing Pugsy against his chest.

"Pugsy likes you!" the princess laughed as her dog began licking Spynosaur's scaly chin. "Maybe I'll keep you as a pet, too!"

Spynosaur raised an eyebrow. He plucked the dog from the princess in a clawed hand and held it up in front of his face.

The dog peered at him.

He peered at the dog.

"Dad, are you OK?" asked Amber. "What—"

KRUNCH!

Everyone froze.

In the long, cold moment of silence that followed, Amber's jaw fell open. She couldn't believe her own eyes ... but then she looked around. Everyone was staring at her dad. They'd all seen it too.

Spynosaur had eaten Pugsy Malone.

Swallowed him, in a single bite.

4.
SPYNOSAUR
GOES ROGUE

"Aaaaaaaaaaaaaaaaaah!" shrieked the princess, pointing a trembling finger at Spynosaur. The whole room glared at him in horror.

"Unthinkable!" gasped the princess's servant. "What have you done?"

"Spyno!" cried Danger Monkey.

"Dad...?" Amber muttered.

"Blast it to smithereens! How could you?" added M11 in disbelief.

"What's everyone looking at?" Spynosaur said, glancing around.

"You ate Pugsy!" the princess wailed. "He ate Pugsy!"

"What on earth are you on about? Pugsy's right here in ... my..." Spynosaur trailed off as he looked down at his clawed hands. The dog was nowhere to be seen.

"Pugsy was a special present to the princess – from the princess!" whimpered the princess's servant, as the princess paced angrily around the throne room.

"I'll blow you up!" she screamed. "I'll blow it *all* up! England and Scotch-land and Welsh-land and all of it!"

"Now 'ang on a— **OOF!**" howled Danger Monkey as the princess kicked him out of the way.

"Your Majesty, wait!" said M11. "I give you my

solemn promise, as the head of Department 6, that any punishment Spynosaur suffers will be a hundred times worse than being blown up, to smithereens or otherwise!"

"Now hang on," said Spynosaur. "I think I'd know if I'd eaten a dog! Especially one as ugly as Pugsy..."

The princess's screams filled the throne room again.

"Do something!" her servant hissed to M11, his hands clamped fretfully round his egg-shaped head.

"I— Spynosaur!" barked M11, her moustache twitching in desperation. "I have put up with your rule-wrecking recklessness for years but you've gone too far this time. You – you leave me no choice..."

Spynosaur's lizard eyes grew wide as M11 took a piece of paper out of her pocket and unfolded it.

CERTIFICATE OF SPYING
This is to certify that

AGENT GAMBIT SPYNOSAUR

Has completed his spy training and is a qualified

SECRET AGENT

With the Right to Spy on whomever (s)he wishes

And save the world where necessary

*

Signed:

"My Certificate of Spying," said Spynosaur as M11 held up the piece of paper. "You wouldn't..."

"You *ate* the mission!" M11 replied, clenching her jaw so hard her teeth squeaked. "Your Right to Spy is revoked. Effective immediately."

With that, she tore the certificate in two.

"You can't!" Amber cried. "Dad didn't mean it! He's a dinosaur! Dinosaurs eat stuff! Even dumb designer dogs!"

"Waaaaah!" the princess howled again.

"It's over, Spynosaur," insisted M11, her moustache drooping. "Hand over your pistol, spy-dentification card, Super Secret Spy Watch™, exploding elbow-pads, imploding handkerchief, tracking tooth, secret skis, inflatable jetpack, Yo-Yo bolas, para-shoes and whatever else you've got hiding in that spy-suit. Under subsection twelve-point-two of the *Big Book of Spies and Spying*, Volume 9, Colour Edition, you will be transported to our high security prison complex beneath Department 6 Headquarters."

"You're putting him in the *Bin*?" howled Amber. "But that's where baddies go!"

"It's all right, Amber," Spynosaur said, without taking his eyes off M11. "Look everyone, I can't tell you what just happened," he continued, "but I'm sure I'm the only one who can find out. So I'm afraid I'll have to politely decline your order."

"You can't decline an order, that's why it's an order!" barked M11. "Danger Monkey, arrest that dinosaur..."

"Sorry, Spyno, this hurts me as much as it does you," Danger Monkey said, taking a pair of hi-tech handcuffs from his belt. "Except for the bit where I put the 'andcuffs on ya – that can really pinch."

"I think I'll pass," Spynosaur said. "Activate elbow flares!"

In an instant, a blinding white light exploded from Spynosaur's elbows.

"My peepers!" Danger Monkey howled, rubbing his eyes. By the time his vision had started to clear, Spynosaur and Amber were floating through the hole in the ceiling, caught in the Dino-soarer's gravity beam.

"He's getting away!" cried the princess's servant as the spies were swallowed inside the Dino-soarer. The jet blasted into the clouds and disappeared, leaving the princess roaring with rage.

"Blast it to smithereens!" M11 growled, tapping her Super Secret Spy Watch™. "To all agents: the fish is out of the bowl! The biscuit is out of the tin! The toilet seat has been left up! *Spynosaur has gone rogue!* Stop him ... by whatever means necessary."

5.
UNDER CONTROL

THE DINO-SOARER
SOARING HIGH ABOVE THE OCEAN

"For the last time, return to headquarters and hand yourself in, that's an order!" M11 commanded over Spynosaur's Super Secret Spy Watch™. "Or I swear by my favourite moustache comb, I will stop at *nothing* to hunt you down."

With one hand on the controls of the Dino-soarer, Spynosaur tore the watch off his wrist with his teeth and crunched it like a cracker.

"Boring conversation anyway," he huffed. From

her seat in the cockpit, Amber watched her dad spit the mangled watch into the Dino-soarer's dustbin.

"So, we're not spies any more?" Amber asked. Her dad didn't reply. After a moment she added, "Do I have to go back to being normal?"

Amber's dad activated the autopilot and turned to her.

"Amber, whatever you think you saw, I didn't eat Pugsy Malone," he said. "I don't do that sort of thing any more."

"Oh, really?" replied Amber. "What about:

"And you nearly ate my pet rabbit, like, three times," Amber added. "It's your *dino-side*, remember?"

"I know I've had issues with my more ferocious facets in the past," Spynosaur replied. "But my dino-side is under control now. You could put me in a *roomful* of pugs and I'd be cooler than a cucumber convention."

"But ... I *saw* you eat him. Everyone did!" Amber said. "You swallowed Pugsy like he was a spy-tamin pill!"

"I know that's what it looked like, but a secret agent can't always trust their spy-sight – sometimes they must trust their *instincts*," said her dad. "What do *your* instincts tell you, Amber?"

Amber closed her eyes and rubbed her temples, the sight of her dad swallowing the princess's dog looping in her brain. She tried to look past it...

"My instincts tell me ... that we're turning round?" she said.

"We are?" said Spynosaur, checking the cockpit controls. Sure enough, the Dino-soarer had changed course.

"M11, you crafty commander-in-chief..." said Spynosaur with an impressed raise of his eyebrow. "Doctor Newfangle, I presume?"

A view screen suddenly extended from the control panel on an articulated metal arm and flashed into life. Moments later a man with an eruption of white hair and thick spectacles appeared on screen.

●○X≡

DEPARTMENT 6

CLASSIFILE   #1687-AAPL

CODE NAME:
DR NEWTOWN NEWFANGLE,
PHD, BTW, ROTFL

>> Chief spy-entist at Department 6. Gadget-maker and science ray specialist. Creates new bodies for agents who have met sorry ends, including the dinosaur that now houses mind of Agent Gambit [SEE: SPYNOSAUR]

DEPARTMENT 6

"I'm so sorry, Spynosaur!" Newfangle declared. "M11 ordered me to take *remote control* of the Dino-soarer. She said after what you'd done to— Well, I couldn't believe it! I said she must be barking up the wrong tree. Sorry! I shouldn't have mentioned barking..."

"But Dad probably didn't eat the dog, maybe!" cried Amber – then immediately regretted not sounding more supportive.

"I wouldn't believe me either," confessed Spynosaur, his dino-mighty muscles straining to turn the Dino-soarer's control wheel. "But just give me a minute and I'll have ... everything ... under ... control...!"

"I'm afraid there's nothing you can do – the Dino-soarer is programmed to bring you back to HQ," said Dr Newfangle. "Everything is under control ... *mine*."

6.
WHEN GADGETS GO BAD
(AKA SPYNOSAUR VS DR NEWFANGLE)

"What do we do? They're going to put you in the Bin, Dad!" Amber cried as the remotely-controlled Dino-soarer conveyed them back to Department 6 headquarters.

"Not before I've had time to crack this case, they're not," said Spynosaur, clenching his fist. "I think it's time to *knuckle* down..."

KRORNCH!

With a mighty punch, Spynosaur drove his fist into the Dino-soarer's controls.

"I had that control panel engraved!" Newfangle cried over the view screen. "*To my greatest creation, Spynosaur. May all your dreams take flight. Hugs, Dr Newfangle. PS Please don't break this one.*"

"Uh, Dad, why are you punching the Dino-soarer?" Amber asked as her dad wrenched out a handful of wires and circuitry from the shattered panel.

"*Wire* not?" Spynosaur replied coolly. He tapped two wires together and they sparked with electricity. "Fix this to that, move that over there, give that a twiddle … yes! I should have manual control of the Dino-soarer in a few seconds."

"Spynosaur, please!" begged Dr Newfangle. "Don't make me activate the Nanny State Protocol!"

"Nanny State Protocol? Never heard of it,"

noted Spynosaur, holding up a bright red wire. "There! All I need to do is connect this to the motherboard and I should have full control of—"

FWUMP!

Spynosaur's para-shoes suddenly opened, engulfing him in several metres of thick cotton.

"Dad!" cried Amber as her dad's sharp claws tore through the material.

"The Nanny State Protocol means I can remotely control your gadgets, Spynosaur!" Newfangle explained guiltily. "*All* of them...!"

Without warning, Spynosaur's secret inflatable jetpack expanded on his back. The gleaming chrome rocket booster burst into life, launching Spynosaur upwards. He collided with the ceiling and bounced off the floor before jetting out of the cockpit and into the Dino-soarer's docking bay.

"Dad!" Amber cried again.

"Conneeeeeect the wiiiiiiire!" Spynosaur shouted,

helplessly ricocheting around the Dino-soarer like a prehistoric pinball. Amber spun round to see the red wire hanging loose from the control panel.

"I'm on it!" she said, but as she leaped into action, Dr Newfangle remotely activated Spynosaur's wrist-mounted spy-net. It shot out of a secret pocket on Spynosaur's sleeve, ensnaring Amber and sending her tumbling to the cockpit floor.

"Aaaambeeeeer!" Spynosaur roared, careening from wall to wall. Finally, he managed to reach behind him, driving both thumb claws into the pumped-up propulsion system on his back. The punctured jetpack let out a loud

FOOOOOOOOOOOOOSH!

as it deflated. Spynosaur plummeted to the floor, bouncing and skidding back into the cockpit. He looked up and spied the loose wire dangling inches in front of his face. He reached out...

"Spynosaur, please stop!" howled Newfangle over the view screen. In desperation, he activated every last gadget in Spynosaur's spy-suit.

The results were dramatic.

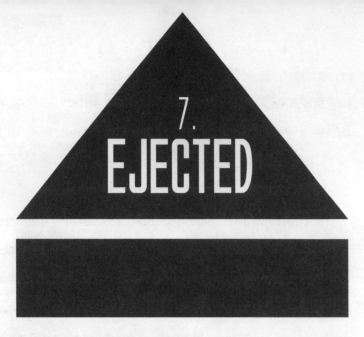

7.
EJECTED

" *RAAARGH!* "

Spynosaur's savage roar filled the air as he tore his spy-suit from his body. Within seconds he'd shredded the hi-tech fabric with his claws.

"Dad, are you OK...?" Amber muttered, still tangled in Spynosaur's spy-net. For a moment, her dad seemed lost to his dino-side. But then Spynosaur blinked and shook his head, as if waking from a bad dream.

"Cucumber cool," he said, brushing the last torn fibres from his shoulders. He untangled Amber from his spy-net, before retrieving her school uniform from a nearby compartment and handing it to her. "Better lose the spy-suit, don't you think?" he added.

"I really am sorry, Spynosaur!" declared Newfangle. "As soon as you're back at HQ I'm sure we can straighten this out..."

"No, *I'm* sorry, Doctor," said Spynosaur, grabbing the view screen in his clawed hands. "I'm afraid you're *breaking* up..."

KRUNCH!

Spynosaur yanked the view screen from its metal arm and threw it to the floor. With an angry grunt, he connected the dangling red wire to the motherboard.

MANUAL CONTROL RESTORED

"You did it!" Amber said, pulling on her school sweater. "Turn us round, before we end up back at headquarters!"

"Not an option, I'm afraid," replied Spynosaur, clambering into the pilot seat. "Even in stealth mode, Newfangle will be able to track us in the Dino-soarer."

"So, what was the point of getting control back?" said Amber, leaping into the co-pilot's seat. Spynosaur activated their harnesses to strap them in.

"Oh, that was just so that I could do *this*," he replied. He flicked a switch on his seat, and the Dino-soarer's canopy ejected from the cockpit. Before Amber knew what was happening, rocket jets ignited beneath her seat and she was blasted out into the sky.

"AAAAAAAAAAAAAA bit of warning next time!" Amber screamed as their jet-powered seats propelled her and Spynosaur clear of the Dino-soarer.

"Where's the fun in that?" Spynosaur said with a grin as they zoomed through the clouds. "Now, pull that cord on your left, will you?"

"This one?" Amber asked, tugging on the red cord fixed to her seat. "Why, what does it doooOOOOOOOO-OOOOOO-OOOOOOO!"

Without warning, Amber was launched out of her ejector seat! As the seat jetted off into the sky, Amber plummeted, the ground getting closer with every second. Before she could work out what her dad had planned, she was closing her eyes and preparing for the end...

"Got you."

Her dad's voice was close and surprisingly calm. Amber opened her eyes and realized that she hadn't hit the ground – her dad, still strapped into his ejector seat, had swooped down and caught her by the leg.

"My ejector seat has its own *ejector seat*?" Amber shrieked as her dad hoisted her into his arms. "What was all that about?"

"Department 6 will be able to trace these ejector seats, too," Spynosaur explained, piloting the seat behind a nearby church and landing in the graveyard. "By splitting them up we stand a better chance of staying undetected."

"And there was no way you could have mentioned that before I FELL OUT OF THE SKY?" Amber howled as her dad deposited her on terra firma.

"As of now, the whole Department is on my tail," her dad replied, clambering out of his ejector seat. "If we're going to stay one step ahead, we need to be unpredictable ... unbelievable ... in short, no more Mr Nice Spy."

8.
SNEAKING PAST SERGEI

⊕ THE VILLAGE OF LITTLE WALLOP

"So, what's the plan?" Amber asked as she and Spynosaur crept through the tree-lined streets of Little Wallop.

"The plan is, there is no plan," her dad replied. "The rules of rule-breaking are about to be broken. I'm going to break rules that haven't even been invented yet. I'm going to break the rules, repair them, then break them again."

"That's super confusing," confessed Amber.

"I'll need some clothes," Spynosaur continued,

darting between two trees. "All my disguises were concealed in my spy-suit – and without a disguise it turns out I look a *lot* like a dinosaur."

"Well, I think Mum still has some of your old clothes from when you were, y'know, human ... but I'm not sure they'll fit any more," said Amber, feeling altogether overwhelmed by the fact they were fugitives from Department 6. "Wait, what about Sergei?"

"I'll deal with your double-in-disguise – no doubt M11's got to him already," said Spynosaur, whipping round a corner into Diggle Drive and ducking behind a postbox. "The important thing is making sure your mum is none the wiser. We can't have her discovering the truth about your double life – or that I live on as this prehistoric ... person."

"But now you're sort of not a secret agent any more," began Amber, "couldn't you tell Mum the *truth*?"

"You mean, admit that I'm a secret agent who, on an ill-fated mission, was tied to a space rocket by criminal mastermind Ergo Ego and fired into the moon but then, through the mysterious power of *spy-ence,* had my human brainwaves transferred into the body of a dinosaur?" said Spynosaur, tiptoeing down the drive to Amber's house. "Out of the question. Your mum hates surprises."

"But—" huffed Amber as they crouched behind her mum's car.

"No buts, Amber – not this time," said her dad. He rested his clawed hands on her shoulders. "Look, as soon as this whole thing is straightened out, life can go back to normal – fighting villains, blowing things up ... all the good stuff. But the only way we can do that is if I clear my name and that means we have to *disappear*, like ghosts or spectres or that one sock you can never find ... but not in the way Department 6 expects, because they'll expect the unexpected! Do you understand?"

"Not really," Amber replied.

"Perfect! I must follow my instincts ... do the opposite of what's expected ... no, the opposite of the opposite of what's expected. I must surprise everyone, especially myself," replied Amber's dad. He clenched his fists. "Let's go!"

Spynosaur and Amber raced over to the house and peered in through the front window. A short, craggy-faced old man, no taller than Amber, was sitting on the sofa, watching television. He was dressed in Amber's school uniform and wearing a red wig that looked just like her own hair.

DEPARTMENT 6

CLASSIFILE   #1984-1-CCCP

CODE NAME:
SERGEI

>> Amber's double-in-disguise.
This undercover agent takes
Amber's place at home and
school when she joins Spynosaur
on missions. (SEE: SPYNOSAUR)

DEPARTMENT 6

As silently as a self-portrait, Spynosaur popped the window's latch with the tip of his tail and nudged it open. In a matter of seconds he poured himself inside, deftly avoiding a small army of windowsill ornaments as he slid into the front room. But, as he ducked behind an armchair, his long tail brushed past a china cat, knocking it off the windowsill.

Amber was barely halfway through the window. She reached in and grabbed the cat a split second before it hit the floor.

Spynosaur and Amber both glanced over at Sergei. He hadn't taken his eyes off the TV. He let out a deep, gravelly chuckle as he watched a cartoon elephant have a sneezing fit in a library.

The spies breathed a silent sigh of relief, and Amber began to climb inside...

"Amber!" called Amber's mum from the kitchen. "Dinner's ready!"

Amber froze, hanging half in and half out of the window. By the time she dared to look at the sofa, Sergei was no longer on it.

"Sergei has eyes in back of head. Not literally, obviously," said a voice like rocks being scraped together. Amber turned to see Sergei standing right in front of her. "But no one can sneak up on Sergei — Sergei is *unsneakupable*," added Sergei, pulling out a Department 6-issue pistol from his skirt. "Now tell me, where is traitor to Department 6? Where is Spynosaur?"

"Amber!" called Amber's mum again. "It's getting cold!"

"Coming!" shouted Amber and Sergei together. In her panic, Amber felt her eyes dart to the armchair. Sergei spun round but it was too late – Spynosaur leaped out from behind the chair and swatted the gun from Sergei's hand. Spynosaur, Amber and Sergei watched the pistol spin through the air as if in slow motion, until:

KRASH!

The gun collided with a bookshelf.

"What was that? Amber!" cried Amber's mum, her voice getting closer.

"Nothing, Mum! Stay there!" Amber yelled, dropping through the window and racing into the kitchen. Out of the corner of her eye, she saw Sergei duck under Spynosaur's legs and leap on to his back, before wrapping his school tie round her dad's throat in an attempt to throttle him.

Ten seconds later, Amber was tucking into fish fingers and chips.

After hastily shovelling down her fish fingers and chips (and a bowl and a half of ice cream) Amber made her excuses to her mum and hurried back into the living room.

No sign of her dad. No sign of Sergei.

Amber raced up to her room.

"Dad...?" Amber whispered, poking her head round the door. The first thing she saw was the unconscious Sergei lying on her bed, defeated in silent combat by Spynosaur. She pushed open the door to find her dad squeezed into a black polo-neck sweater and a pair of grey trousers, the seat of which he'd punctured so he could poke out his tail.

"You found your old clothes?" Amber said.

"You were right — everything's a bit snug now I'm a dinosaur," replied Spynosaur, straining the sweater's seams with a flex of his prehistoric pectorals. "Of course, even with my achingly impressive spy skills I won't fool anyone into thinking I'm human – not without *this*..."

Spynosaur whipped off Sergei's wig and popped it on top of his own head, flattening it into a neat side-parting.

"Riiiight," said Amber with an eye roll. As she watched Spynosaur put one of her woolly hats on to Sergei's head, she started to feel less and less sure about his plan not to have a plan ... but since the alternative was her dad being locked away forever, she kept her doubts to herself – including the possibility that he really did eat Pugsy Malone. "So, now what?" she asked.

"Sergei's too much of a pro to blow his cover," said Spynosaur. "When he wakes up he'll be sure to keep your mum in the dark about all of this."

"And you're *sure* Department 6 won't be able to find us?" Amber added.

"There's only one spy who might have had the skills necessary to track me down – *Agent A55*," mused Spynosaur, opening the bedroom window. "But since an ill-fated mission involving a pit of secret-agent-eating snakes, A55's tracking days are over ... as are her days of being alive."

"OK, so now what?" said Amber with a shrug.

"Now," replied Spynosaur. "We *disappear*."

10.
JET SETTER
(AKA THE FATE OF AGENT A55)

 DEPARTMENT 6 HEADQUARTERS
BENEATH THE NATURAL HISTORY
MUSEUM, LONDON

"NEWFANGLE!"

M11 burst into the bustling Department 6 control centre, her cries echoing around the wide, brightly lit room. Black-clad agents fled for cover as M11 strode past them, with Danger Monkey following close behind.

"Clear a path!" the monkey cried. "Angry boss comin' through!"

M11 swept into Dr Newfangle's laboratory and glanced around. Every corner of the lab was piled high with hi-tech gadgets and equipment, but the middle of the room was empty ... except for Dr Newfangle crouching on the floor with his knees pulled up to his chin.

"Do get up, Doctor," M11 said stiffly. "It's no use hiding behind an *invisible* car."

"Ah," Dr Newfangle muttered. He pressed a button on his Super Secret Spy Watch™ and a black sports car materialized in front of them. Newfangle sidled out from behind it, looking sheepish. "H-hello, M11," he squeaked. "May I say your moustache is looking particularly well-combed today...?"

"Blast it to smithereens, Newfangle, I gave you the Nanny State Protocol!" M11 roared. "Full access to Spynosaur's Dino-soarer, his gadgets ... his *underwear*, for goodness' sake! And by the time I get back from Canada, he's evaded capture and disappeared off the face of the Earth!"

"Disappeared?" Newfangle repeated.

"Sergei just reported in – Spynosaur showed up at the Gambit house," M11 explained, her moustache twitching angrily. "He took a disguise and Sergei's best wig! He's gone deep cover!"

"Vanished, like my childhood teddy bear, Captain Cuddles," added Danger Monkey. "Where are ya, Captain? Come back t' me!"

"But I can fix this," insisted Dr Newfangle. "You see—"

"*No one* can fix this," M11 snapped. "The only agent who might have been able to track Spynosaur down was A55, but since she took a nosedive into that pit of secret-agent-eating snakes—"

"Mission 147: *Just for the Snake of it*," added a forlorn Danger Monkey.

"—She's gone, and with her, our chance of finding Spynosaur," M11 howled. "When the princess of Canada finds out we've let Pugsy's killer get away, it'll mean war!"

"M11, please listen!" begged Dr Newfangle. "You see, ever since Ergo Ego fired Agent Gambit into the moon, I have taken the liberty of recording the brainwaves of every single agent in the Department, in case something should ... happen to them."

"Why you lookin' at me when you say that?" snarled Danger Monkey. "D'you think I wanted to end up as a monkey? *Anyone* could've fallen into that pool of piranhas! 'Ow was I supposed to know they were goin' to eat me?"

"So, when A55 met her sorry end, I transferred her brainwaves into a *new* body," Newfangle continued, ignoring Danger Monkey's rant. "A body created by science rays!"

"Ugh, you and that science-ray machine," groaned M11, rubbing her eyes with a finger and thumb. "This place already resembles a zoo thanks to your *spy-ence* experiments — former spies turned into monkeys ... moles ... fish... For a week, I had a *fruit fly spy* buzzing around my office..."

"And now, there's *me*," said a voice as cool as an ice cube inside another ice cube. Sitting on top of the sports car was an Irish setter with a reddish-brown coat and long ears that hung below her chin.

"Wait ... *A55*?" gasped M11.

CLASSIFILE #BUS-A55

CODE NAME:
JET SETTER
(AKA AGENT A55)

>> Expert tracker and strategist. Able to find anyone, anywhere, any time. Relentless and determined. Not one to let an unfortunate encounter with a pit of secret-agent-eating snakes get her down. Loves the finer things in life. And dog food.

DEPARTMENT
6

"At your service," replied the dog, loping down the bonnet and on to the floor. "But since Newfangle has been *hounding* me to pick a new code name, perhaps you'd better call me *Jet Setter*."

"If you can find Spynosaur, agent, I'll get you a ball and a bone," snarled M11.

"Deal," Jet Setter replied. "You see, Spynosaur knows that we know he knows we're looking for him but he doesn't know that *I* know he knows we know he knows. He'll be the first to find the last place we'd think of looking, but he knows we know that, too, so he wouldn't think of being the first to hide in the last place we'd think of looking first ... and he knows we know that."

"Stop stallin', you confusin' canine!" snapped Danger Monkey, squaring up to Jet Setter. "Spyno's saved my life more times than I've eaten bananas and I owe him that. But when he scoffed the princess's pooch, Spynosaur brought shame upon Department 6! Also, M11 said if I bring 'im in she'll make me Number One Spy. Now, do you know 'ow to find Spyno or not?"

"Oh, I've *already* found him," said Jet Setter. "Warm up a jet ... it's time to snare ourselves a Spynosaur."

11.
HIDING IN PLAIN SIGHT
(AKA THE FÊTE OF SPYNOSAUR)

LITTLE WALLOP CHURCH BELFRY,
LITTLE WALLOP

"So just to be clear, this is what you call disappearing?"

Amber and her dad were huddled in the dusty, cold belfry of Little Wallop Church, surrounded by church bells and cobwebs.

"It's been two days and we haven't gone *anywhere*," Amber added. "I mean, I can still see my house from here ... how is this a plan?"

"The plan is, no plan!" her dad replied giddily, holding his wig in one hand and flattening the hair with the other. "Even the most devil-may-care maverick wouldn't stay in the last place they were seen. Hiding in Little Wallop makes no sense, and that's exactly the sort of thing no one will expect."

"I was sort of thinking we'd go to Mexico..." confessed Amber with a sigh. She brushed a cobweb out of her hair and tried to get comfy on an unforgiving wooden beam. "Anyway, how are we going to make people believe you didn't eat Pugsy Malone if we're stuck in here?"

"*Make* people believe— Wait, do you *still* think I ate the princess's dog?" asked Spynosaur, replacing the wig on his head.

"No, I mean, maybe — I mean, I don't know!" Amber confessed. She tried to stand but ended up banging her head on a church bell. The bell TONG-ed loudly. Her dad ducked under the bell to give her a hug.

"It's confusing for me, too," Spynosaur admitted, giving Amber a squeeze. "My brain is telling me I'm guilty as charged. But I can't afford to trust my brain — I have to trust my instincts."

"Which means we're hiding in a roomful of bells, just across the road from my own bedroom? *Great*," Amber grumbled sarcastically, squirming out of the hug. "Nothing makes sense any more..."

"Sense...? Of course! Good thinking, Amber," said Spynosaur, leaping to his feet. "Hiding here makes no sense, but the only thing that makes even less sense is *not* hiding. We should be hiding out there, in broad daylight!"

"What? That's not what I meant!" Amber cried. "At least, I don't think it is..."

"It's madness! M11 will never see it coming!" Spynosaur declared, clambering across the church beams to the nearest window. "Also, didn't your mum mention a village fête? Could be fun!"

"The fête? Wait!" Amber said. "What if Mum goes with Sergei? She might see us!"

"Sergei hates organized fun, he'll do anything to get out of going," replied Amber's dad. "Or they might both show up and our secret will be revealed to the world! Who knows?"

"But—!" Amber blurted as her dad threw himself out of the belfry window. She shook her head, shrugged, and followed him into the outside world.

The streets of Little Wallop were busier than Amber had ever seen them. It seemed like the whole village had turned up for the fête, and half the neighbouring villages besides. Quaint, bunting-covered stalls lined the main road, selling jams and cakes and trinkets of no discernible value. At one end of the street, a prim woman with a clipboard judged an Excellent Egg competition;

at the other, a muddy-booted man mumbled and waved rosettes at a pen filled with potential prize pigs. But the largest crowd had gathered on the village green to watch a pair of medieval-looking "knights" in armour and bright plumes jousting on horseback.

And, in the middle of it all, wandering through the crowds was a dinosaur in a wig.

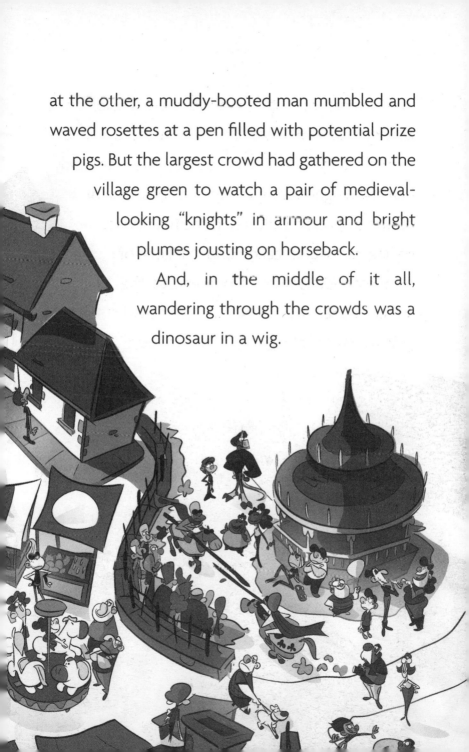

"This is bonkers like conkers!" Amber said, hoping against hope that no one saw through her dad's flimsy disguise. "It's like we're *asking* to get caught..."

"Time to trust your instincts, Amber," replied Spynosaur, stopping to buy cupcakes from a young woman with blue hair. He handed Amber a strawberry-topped cake. "Especially if your instincts defy logic, common sense and everything your spy training has taught you."

"That might be the most confusing thing you've ever said to me," Amber huffed, stuffing the cupcake in her mouth in one go. "And you once told me to put my head in a man-eating crocodile's mouth."

"Which *distracted* the crocodile just long enough for me to put it in a sleeper hold!" said Spynosaur proudly. "Trust me, Amber, if we're going to find out what happened back in Canada, we're going to have to throw thinking out of the window. All we have to do is wait for the answer to reveal itself ... and not get caught, obviously. But there's no way anyone could possibly find me, when—"

"Spynosaur!"

At the cry, Spynosaur and Amber spun round and scanned the crowds with their spy-sight. "Down here," the voice said. Spynosaur looked down. In front of him stood a large dog with a glossy red-brown coat.

"It can't be..." Spynosaur muttered.

"Oh, but it is," said Jet Setter. "Found you."

12.
SURROUNDED

"A55, is that really you?" Spynosaur cried, dropping his cupcake in surprise.

"It's Jet Setter now, darling," replied the dog, examining Spynosaur through intense brown eyes. "So, is that a wig or did a cat die on your head?"

"You're not quite the woman I once knew, either," replied Spynosaur, adjusting his makeshift toupee. "Still a redhead, though. I see..."

"Da-ad, we need to go...!" hissed Amber, nudging Spynosaur with her elbow. "They found us!"

"Actually, I found you," Jet Setter replied. "Credit where it's due, Spynosaur — you led me on a merry chase..."

"What chase? We didn't go anywhere," Amber huffed.

"I wasn't about to make it easy for you, Setter," Spynosaur said with a raise of his eyebrow. "Even if I didn't know you were after me."

"And I wasn't going to let you slip away, darling," said Jet Setter. "You see, I knew you didn't know about my return — and I knew you knew I knew you didn't know I knew you knew I knew you didn't know. But I knew your plan was to plan not to plan so I planned a plan based on a plan not to plan and ran with the plan. You thought you could not think — instinct, I think — I think you think you thought your way through was not to think and when I thought it through I thought it must be true, that you, yes you, were the sort of man to abandon a plan and then I knew, I knew I'd find you ... here, only a few metres from your former home, dressed in a wig at a village fête!"

"Well, I can't argue with your logic," Spynosaur admitted.

"When Jet Setter's on your tail, there's ... nowhere ... to..." began Jet Setter, gazing down at Spynosaur's discarded cupcake. After a moment, she picked up the cake in her jaws and wolfed it down.

"Sorry, that was disgusting – I'm afraid I'm still getting used to being a dog," she said. "But then I'm not the only agent with a troublesome *appetite*, am I, Spynosaur?"

"I'm totally innocent," insisted Spynosaur. "I just have to work out why I'm not guilty."

"Save your defence for M11, darling ... we're here to take you to the Bin," replied Jet Setter.

"'We'?" Spynosaur repeated. His eyes darted left, then right. Then he saw them.

The prim woman with a clipboard.

The muddy-booted pig judge.

The blue-haired cupcake seller.

The two jousting knights.

The two knights' horses.

All seven of them were secret agents.

Spynosaur was surrounded.

"Diabolical," Spynosaur muttered, gazing into the middle distance. "I was too busy trusting my instincts to see what was in front of my face."

"They're *everywhere* ... Dad, what do we do?" whispered Amber as the agents closed in. "We can't actually *fight* Department 6, can we?"

"You should listen to your daughter, Spynosaur," said Jet Setter. She cocked her head towards Spynosaur's sidekick. "I've been meaning to ask, Amber — did you *see* your dad eat poor Pugsy Malone with your own eyes?"

"Yeah, but—" she muttered.

"Well, so did everyone else in that throne room," Jet Setter added quickly. "It's time to face facts — Spynosaur betrayed Department 6. Your father is a *traitor*. Unless he has another explanation?"

Amber looked up at her dad, desperately hoping

that he had exactly that.

"I'm sorry, Amber ... all I have is my instincts," said Spynosaur. "And my instincts tell me I didn't eat that dog."

"Time to choose a side, sidekick," said Jet Setter. "What do *your* instincts tell you?"

"My instincts?" Amber began. She remembered seeing her dad swallowing the princess of Canada's dog. She remembered thinking nothing made sense.

Then she struck an impressive fighting pose and clenched her fists.

"My instincts tell me *no one* calls my dad a traitor," she said. "It's time to ninja-kick some secret agents."

13. FÊTE FIGHT
(AKA SPYNOSAUR VS THE AGENTS)

SPYNOSAUR IS USED TO FIGHTING VILLAINY AND CRIME

BUT HE'S NEVER BEEN THE BADDIE IN HIS OWN SPY-TASTIC RHYME!

DID HE SWALLOW PUGSY? IS HE MONSTROUS TO THE CORE?

IS HIS DESTINY TO BE A REALLY ROTTEN DINOSAUR?

SPYNOSAUR!

14.
TANKS BUT NO TANKS
(AKA SPYNOSAUR VS DANGER MONKEY)

"Well, that was disappointing," sighed Jet Setter, as the last of the secret agents slumped to the ground. She watched Spynosaur jump down from his horse, and added, "I don't suppose you'd consider just *surrendering*, darling?"

"I'm afraid not – I'm pretty sure I'm one important revelation away from clearing my name," said Spynosaur.

"I thought you might say that," she said coolly. "That's why I brought *him*."

A low, bone-shaking rumble filled the air and the ground began to shake. As Jet Setter retreated to a safe distance, screams of panic rang out around Little Wallop. A few seconds later, the horrified crowds scattered, racing in every direction.

"I'll cramp yer style! I'll upset yer apple cart! I'll throw a spanner in yer works!" came a cry.

"Is that who I think it is...?" said Amber, spinning round.

Then they saw it — a huge, armoured tank with a cannon mounted on its roof. Danger Monkey's tiny head poked out of the tank's turret as it rolled over cars and crashed through stalls.

"Danger Monkey, stop!" Spynosaur cried as the tank headed straight towards them. "Don't give in to fierce loyalty, blind ambition and/or monkey business!"

"I ain't stoppin' 'til I've stopped stoppin' you!" Danger Monkey replied. "Nobody makes a monkey out of Department 6!"

With that, Danger Monkey swung the tank's huge cannon in Spynosaur's direction.

"He wouldn't!" Amber blurted.

"He might..." Spynosaur replied.

He did.

Spynosaur and his sidekick leaped into the air as Danger Monkey fired. The cupcake stall exploded in a shower of crumbs and frosting.

"'Old still, Spyno!" Danger Monkey insisted.

BOM-BOOM!

This time, a table filled with plump prize marrows was reduced to a pulpy vegetable mess. As Amber dived for cover behind the Excellent Egg stall, Spynosaur sprang into the air once again, spiralling and spinning until he landed squarely on top of the tank.

"*Danger Monkey, stop!*" Spynosaur roared, the tank's cannon swinging towards the egg stall. He grabbed hold of the cannon's barrel and wrenched it with all his dino-might. The seams in his sweater split as his spy-ence-made muscles strained to breaking point. Then, with a final heave, Spynosaur bent the barrel until it pointed straight up into the sky.

"You seem a little bent out of shape, Danger Monkey!" Spynosaur boomed. "I bet you couldn't hit a dinosaur with a meteor!"

"I'll show you! I'll blast you back to the early Cretaceous Period!" roared Danger Monkey.

He disappeared inside the turret and reached for the fire button.

With a **BOM!** the armour-piercing missile fired ... but thanks to the tank's bent barrel, the missile streaked up into the air, blasting high into the sky, until finally, it spluttered to a stop and began to fall.

"*Tanks* for putting me through my paces, Danger Monkey, but I really must be off," said Spynosaur with a grin. With his mighty legs, he jumped clear, as the missile plummeted back to earth ... straight towards Danger Monkey's tank.

15.
SURRENDER

The force of the explosion blew Spynosaur through the air, landing with a **KRUMCH!** on top of the Excellent Egg stall.

"Dad!" Amber cried, clambering out from beneath the shattered stall. Her dad dragged himself to his feet, covered in smashed eggs and the odd rosette.

"Don't worry, I'm *yolk*-ay," Spynosaur replied, picking pieces of shell off his scaly skin.

"Da-ad," sighed Amber.

A moment later, a singed and smoking Danger Monkey crawled out from the tank's escape hatch. "Tell ... you what..." he coughed, too battered to even put out the fire on the tip of his tail. "Let's call it ... a draw..."

"Not a chance!" Amber yelled defiantly. "My dad can take whatever you throw at him. Bring it on! My instincts tell me he didn't eat Pugsy Malone, and I won't stop fighting 'til we prove it! No surrender... right, Dad? ...Dad?"

Amber turned to see her dad pluck the only remaining unbroken egg from the ground.

"That's it..." Spynosaur muttered, peering at the egg. "*That's* what I've been missing all this time! That's the important revelation I've been waiting for!"

EGG

EGG-SHAPED HEAD
(PRINCESS OF CANADA'S SERVANT)

EGG-SHAPED HEAD
(CRIMINAL MASTERMIND)

With that, Spynosaur plucked his wig from his head and threw it to the ground. Then he raised his hands high in the air.

"Dad ... what are you doing?" Amber whispered nervously.

"Surrendering," Spynosaur replied, his arms aloft. "I am Spynosaur – the world's greatest secret agent – and I surrender!"

16.
LOCKED UP

"THE BIN" HIGH SECURITY PRISON, BENEATH DEPARTMENT 6 HEADQUARTERS, LONDON

Three hours later, Spynosaur was being led down a stark, grey-white corridor by armed guards. He was dressed in a Department 6 issue jumpsuit with his clawed hands cuffed and had a metal muzzle clamped over his jaws. The guards ushered the world's greatest secret agent through a twisting complex of underground tunnels to a starkly lit, grey-walled prison cell.

As an agent nudged Spynosaur nervously inside, a tiny black mole scurried up to his cell.

The mole was no more than a few inches long, with glasses perched on his pink snout and carrying a tiny control pad.

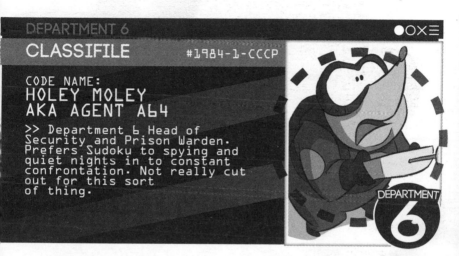

DEPARTMENT 6   ●○X≡
CLASSIFILE   #1984-1-CCCP

CODE NAME:
HOLEY MOLEY
AKA AGENT A64
>> Department 6 Head of
Security and Prison Warden.
Prefers Sudoku to spying and
quiet nights in to constant
confrontation. Not really cut
out for this sort
of thing.

DEPARTMENT
6

"S-sorry, Spynosaur! I hate to— I mean, I'm just doing my— I mean..." Holey Moley whimpered as he pressed a button on the control pad. A wide glass door slid shut, securing Spynosaur's cell.

"Uhgraygull glarsh?" he grunted though the muzzle.

"I – I beg your pardon?" said Holey Moley meekly.

He pressed another button on his control pad and Spynosaur's muzzle popped open and clanged to the ground.

"I said, *unbreakable glass*?" said Spynosaur, tapping the impenetrable glass door with the tip of his tail. "No point in trying to break out of here, I presume?"

"Oh, dear me, no! This glass is tougher than the Department 6 entrance exam ... and it can only be opened by, well, me," replied Holey Moley, waving his control pad. He glanced at the cell behind him. "I – I did what you asked," he added in a whisper. "But if you don't mind me— What I mean to say is, *why*? Why ask for a prison cell opposite Ergo Ego?"

"Instinct," Spynosaur replied. "Now, where's my—"

"Dad!"

Spynosaur peered through the door of his cell

to see Amber racing down the corridor, followed by M11 and the rest of the Department 6 high command – Dr Newfangle, Jet Setter and a battered and bandaged Danger Monkey.

"Behave yourself, sidekick," barked M11 as Amber pressed herself up against Spynosaur's cell door. "Don't make me regret letting you down here..."

"You're all crazy like daisies!" Amber roared. "My dad isn't bad!"

"We all saw what happened, even if Spynosaur won't admit his crime," said M11 with a heavy heart. She glanced awkwardly at Spynosaur. "Confessing does not excuse what you did, agent — but it does mean we'll give you comfier pillows."

"Don't bother," said Spynosaur, giving Amber a wink. "I'll think you'll find I have everything I need..."

"Do you stupid heads have to accompany me every time I go to the toilet?"

The cry rang out across the corridors of the Bin. Everyone turned to see Ergo Ego stamping towards them, dressed in a prison jumpsuit and accompanied by a pair of armed guards. "You know I can't 'go' with you waiting outside! What, do you think I'm going to try and escape down the U-bend? Stupid heads! I've got a good mind to—"

Ego stopped in his tracks. He looked past Amber and M11 and the rest of Department 6 as if they were invisible.

"Do my eyes deceive me?" Ego shrieked as the guards ushered him inside his cell. "Spynosaur, locked up like a common criminal? Yes! You stupid heads have finally done something right!"

"Shut up, stinker!" Amber roared, her fists clenched and shaking. "You tied my dad to a space rocket and fired him into the moon! I should ninja-kick you right in the villainy!"

"Amber, it's all right," said Spynosaur. "I'm where I have to be … where I *need* to be. I belong here."

"But you didn't do it!" Amber began.

"Enough," M11 snapped. "Even if Spynosaur's capture has averted World War Three, I'm still going to be cleaning up this mess 'til Doomsday. As hard as it is to admit, Spynosaur is a criminal … he belongs in the Bin. And, as of tomorrow, we're pulling Sergei out of number thirteen Diggle Drive."

"Wait, what? But—" Amber began.

"No buts, Amber – you're going back to being a normal schoolgirl," M11 concluded. "Your spying days are over."

17.
ERGO EGO'S BIG BOX OF FANTASTICALLY FOOLPROOF INGENIOUS IDEAS TO DEFINITELY DEFEAT SPYNOSAUR

"M11, would you give me a moment with my daughter?" said Spynosaur as Amber hung her head.

M11 let out a long, exasperated sigh that faded into silence as she and the rest of Department 6 left Amber alone in the corridor. Amber knelt down on the floor outside her dad's cell.

"I don't know about you stupid heads, but I'm enjoying this no end!" squealed Ergo Ego from inside his cell. "So tell me, Spynosaur, what did you do to end up in here? Blow up one historical landmark too many?"

"You know exactly what I did, Ego — or rather, what I didn't do," said Spynosaur, grinding his sharp teeth. "Back in Little Wallop, the last unbroken egg at the Excellent Egg stall reminded me of the egg-headed servant in the princess of Canada's throne room. The glasses and false beard were a stroke of genius, but they weren't enough to fool me ... the servant was you, Ergo Ego!"

"What are you blathering about?" replied Ego, scratching his egg-shaped head. "Sounds like you've taken one too many hits to the noggin, Spynosaur."

"I don't get it — how could Ego be in the princess's palace if he's in the Bin?" Amber asked.

"I'm not sure ... but I know an illusion when I don't see one," replied Spynosaur. "Do you remember when Ego used his *brain fog* on us and made us think we were in prehistoric times?"

"Mission 45: *Mind Games and McGuffins*?" Amber replied.

"Ooh, I remember! That was one of my top-ten mind manipulations!" Ego declared, clapping his hands excitedly. "I made you stupid heads think you were fighting dinosaurs!"

"Shut up," Amber growled. "No one cares about your stupid brain fog, making people think they've seen something ... they ... haven't..."

Amber trailed off as her eyes grew wide. She looked at her dad, who smiled back at her and nodded.

"Ego's brain fog!" Amber declared. "What if he used it back in the Canadian palace? That would mean—"

"–That the whole thing was an illusion," concluded Spynosaur. "I didn't eat Pugsy Malone – Ego's brain fog just made it look like I did."

"Stinker!" Amber growled, rounding on Ergo Ego. "You framed my dad!"

"As much as I would love that to be true," Ego confessed, "how could I possibly carry out such a plan when I've been here the whole— Wait, did you say 'eat'?" Ego leaped to his feet. "That was my idea!"

"So you admit it!" Amber yelled.

"They say confession is good for the soul, Ego," declared Spynosaur victoriously. "Now, if you could repeat what you just said to M11, I can clear my name and get back to being the world's greatest secret—"

"No, I mean it was one of my *unused* ideas!" Ego interrupted. "From my Big Box of Fantastically Foolproof Ingenious Ideas to Definitely Defeat

Spynosaur!" He raced over to his bed and retrieved a small and battered cardboard box from underneath. He opened the box and rifled through it, tossing out pieces of paper of varying shapes and sizes.

"Wait, here it is!" Ego said at last, holding up a piece of crumpled paper. "Plan 23: Spyno-jaw! Use brain fog to make everyone think that Spynosaur has eaten something or someone he shouldn't..."

"Stinker!" Amber cried again.

"But don't you see? I never got to carry out my plan because you locked me up ... which means someone stole my idea!" roared Ego. "How dare they! A villain's evil schemes are not to be shared like nibbles at a party or passed around like ... nibbles at a party! This is criminal!"

"Diabolical," snarled Spynosaur, stroking his scaly chin. "But if Ego didn't frame me, then who did?"

"Oh no," Ego gasped, the colour suddenly draining from his egg-shaped head. "It's him."

"Him? Him who?" said Spynosaur, pressing himself against the door of his cell. "Tell me!"

"It's Hugo," Ego said again, a shiver running down his spine. "It's my son."

18.
WHEN YOU'VE GOT TO GO...

"You have a son, Ego?" Spynosaur gasped.

"Hugo Ego!" Ergo Ego replied, stamping around his prison cell. "And that thieving diabolical plan-stealer stole my diabolical plan!"

"No, but seriously ... you have a son?" Amber repeated in disbelief.

"Oh, I'm sorry, I didn't realize only good guys are allowed to make time for a family!" Ego sneered defensively. "What, do you think I just sit around all day plotting the downfall of my enemies?"

"Well ... yeah," Amber replied with a shrug.

"Criminal masterminds need companionship, too, you know," Ego huffed. "Hugo's mother and I were happy, for a time ... specifically, the time before we had Hugo. After that it was a waking nightmare. Hugo was devising diabolical plots while he was still in nappies."

"Wait, you're trying to tell me it was your son who framed me?" asked Spynosaur.

"He's always stealing my ideas!" tutted Ego. "I didn't even want him to be a villain – I mean, who wants competition from their own son? – but his mother thought evildoing would be character-building. He took to it like a duck to water ... or a criminal to crime."

"If this story was any more made-up, you'd be wearing lipstick," Amber scoffed. "You don't believe this, do you, Dad?"

Spynosaur swished his tail thoughtfully as he

paced around his cell.

"I have to trust my instincts ... and they tell me Ego is telling the truth," he said at last. "It seems Hugo Ego is the key to clearing my name ... and I have a new arch-enemy."

"What? No, *I'm* your arch-enemy!" Ego protested. "I'm your unforgettable nemesis, whose dastardly deeds will haunt your nightmares forever!"

"Tell me where to find him, Ego," said Spynosaur. "Where do I find Hugo?"

"I'll take you to him — oh wait, we're both in prison," Ego replied sarcastically.

"Not for long!" declared Amber. "Do you really think my dad would let himself be captured and locked in the Bin without a plan to escape?"

"Ah," said Spynosaur, tapping his cell's unbreakable door with a clawed finger. "That."

"Da-ad, seriously?" said Amber in disbelief. "You don't have an escape plan?"

"No plans at all! That's my new thing…" said Spynosaur with an awkward shrug.

"Ha!" Ego laughed. "Being accompanied to the toilet doesn't seem so bad when I get to mock you for the rest of your stupid life!"

"Good point, Ego," said Spynosaur. "When you've got to go, you've got to go."

ONE MINUTE LATER

"I need the toilet!"

Spynosaur's cry rang out. Within seconds Holey Moley and three armed security guards were racing down the corridor towards his prison cell. Amber sat in the corridor, her head in her hands.

"The 'I need the toilet' trick? Really?" she whispered. "Even my teacher wouldn't fall for this…"

"The call of nature is nothing to be ashamed

about, Amber!" Spynosaur declared loudly. "Especially when it's a number two!"

"Da-ad," Amber groaned.

"He's lying, you stupid heads!" snapped Ergo Ego. "He's going to escape! Also, if you'd put toilets in the cells this really wouldn't be an issue..."

"That — that's not true, is it, Spynosaur?" Holey Moley squeaked, his clawed finger hovering over the unlock button on his control pad. "You're not secretly planning to attempt a dramatic escape, are you?"

"I'm desperate! For the loo, I mean," replied Spynosaur. "And look, there are four of you and one of me — what's the worst that can happen?"

"Let's find out!" said Amber. As quick as a flash, she leaned over and pressed the control pad.

The door swung open.

THE WORST THAT CAN HAPPEN

Having dispatched the guards, Spynosaur locked them in his cell with Holey Moley.

"Oh dear..." Holey Moley whimpered. "How – how are you going to find the toilet now?"

"I'll hold it in," Spynosaur replied with a wink. He turned to Ergo Ego, still locked in his cell. "You're coming with me, Ego. Time to find your son."

"The only way out of here is through Department 6 headquarters, you stupid head," Ego sneered. "There are a hundred more agents between here and freedom!"

"Exactly," said Spynosaur, producing a pistol that he'd pilfered from one of the security guards. He nodded to Amber, who used the control pad to open the door to Ego's cell.

"What are you doing?" Ego blurted as Spynosaur stepped inside his cell and offered up his pistol.

Ego waited a moment, before grabbing the gun like a hungry squirrel snatching a nut.

"You stupid stupid head!" Ego bellowed, pressing the pistol against Spynosaur's forehead. "You have handed me my victory!"

"No, I've handed you a choice," Spynosaur replied. "You can take revenge ... or you can escape."

19.
ESCAPE FROM DEPARTMENT 6

⊙ DEPARTMENT 6 HEADQUARTERS

BLAM!
BLAM!

"Don't move your muscles, stupid heads! Diabolical criminal mastermind coming through!" cried Ergo Ego, the sound of gunshots echoing around the Department 6 control centre. He jabbed the pistol into Spynosaur's back as the scaly secret agent and his sidekick stumbled into the room, their arms held high.

"You fiend, Ego. Let us go!" Spynosaur declared

dramatically as a dozen agents leaped from their desks. "You may have escaped from your cell, overpowered the guards and inexplicably taken me and my sidekick hostage, but you'll never get away with this!"

"Yeah, give it up, you dumb-brained, eggy-head stinker!" Amber added.

"Do we really need the name-calling?" Ego whispered under his breath. "I agreed to go along with your stupid escape plan, didn't I?"

A moment later, M11 burst out of her office with Dr Newfangle, Jet Setter and a bandaged Danger Monkey in tow.

"Blast it to smithereens, get back in the Bin this instant!" M11 barked.

"Do what she says, or I'll pick yer nose!" added Danger Monkey, limping towards them on tiny crutches. "I'll floss yer teeth! I'll clean out yer earwax!"

"Everybody, back!" said Spynosaur. "Ego is a man on edge! Clearly, he's unhinged..."

"Crazy like a daisy!" added Amber. "Bonkers like conkers! Loopy like a rollercoaster!" Amber shouted.

"I think they get the message!" Ego whispered. "Can we hurry this along?"

"You should give Ego what he wants — namely, a clear path to the hangar and a jet plane," concluded Spynosaur. As Ego edged them through the control room, Jet Setter leaped over a desk and jumped down in front of them.

"Are you seriously suggesting Ergo Ego broke out of his cell, released you, and then managed to take you prisoner?" she asked, eyeing Spynosaur suspiciously.

"I'm having an off day," replied Spynosaur.

"Enough talk, you stupid heads!" insisted Ergo Ego. "You'll do as I say, or else! Allow me to explain..."

Ego inexplicably produced a microphone from his prison jumpsuit, and so began:

ERGO EGO'S RIGHT ROTTEN RAP

I'm so bad that I give myself detention

All those other criminals, they don't deserve a mention

I'm the main offender! I'm crooked like the banks

My evil plots are tighter than your granny's favourite Spanx!

I'm so bad I'm getting badder just by spitting out this rhyme

I'll be bad again tomorrow 'cause I'm evil all the time

I'm so good at being evil! I'm so right at being wrong!

So you'd better do my bidding, 'cause I'm saying it in song!

"Well, he's convinced me," said Dr Newfangle.

"Blast it to smithereens! I won't condone violence unless I have ordered it!" barked M11.

"Everyone, get back! Give Ego a clear path to the hangar. Doctor Newfangle, do we have a jet ready to fly?"

"Of course!" Newfangle replied, glancing over to his computer. Then he gave M11 a less-than-subtle wink. "Everything is ... under control."

"Tell me, Doctor, is that the computer you used to take control of the Dino-soarer?" Spynosaur asked.

"Oh, yes!" Newfangle replied. "I can remote-control all of the Department's jets from right here! Why do you ask?"

"No reason," replied Spynosaur. In a lightning-swift move, Spynosaur plucked the pistol from Ergo Ego's hand and took aim.

BLAM!

The gunshot left Newfangle's computer in smoking ruins. Before Ergo Ego even knew what was happening, Spynosaur handed back the pistol.

"He made me do it," Spynosaur said, raising his arms in the air.

"Something doesn't smell right," Jet Setter mused as Ego ushered Spynosaur and Amber towards the hangar. She called after him. "You know I'll find you, Spynosaur! Wherever you go, you know I know you know I know I'll find you!"

"Actually, I'm counting on it," Spynosaur said under his breath.

20.
THE VOLCANO

○ HIGH ABOVE THE OCEAN
   IN A DEPARTMENT 6 JET PLANE

The jet had been in the air for four hours. The sky outside the cockpit window was now dark and speckled with stars. Amber had spent the trip sandwiched in the cockpit between Spynosaur and Ergo Ego. She had never been in such close proximity to a pair of enemies for this long.

It was surprisingly annoying.

"I can't believe Hugo stole my ideas!" Ego howled for the eighteenth time that trip. "Me!

Ergo Ego, the world's most diabolical criminal mastermind..."

"I'd say you've been demoted," Spynosaur said. "Your son sounds like just the sort of arch-enemy the world's greatest secret agent needs."

"You were fired! You're the world's greatest unemployed dinosaur!" scoffed Ego. "And you only know about Hugo because of me, the world's most diabolical criminal mastermind."

"And yet the only reason you're not still in the Bin is because of me, the world's greatest secret agent," Spynosaur replied.

"And the only reason you managed to escape from Department 6 is because of me, the world's most diabolical criminal mastermind!" Ego hissed.

"Sto-op, both of you!" Amber snapped. She climbed out of her seat and moved to the back of the cockpit in frustration. She leaned huffily against the wall, her shoulder accidentally pressing against a hidden panel. With a CLUNK-VRRR! the panel slid aside to reveal a secret compartment filled with spy equipment. "Secret gadget stuff!" she said with glee. She rummaged around and plucked what looked like a biro from the compartment. "Laser pen, X-Ray specs ... there's even a pair of para-shoes in here! Hey, Dad, I've got a plan – let's kit ourselves out with all this spy gear and—"

"No plans," said Spynosaur firmly. "If Hugo Ego is as diabolical as I think he is, he'll be expecting us to arrive prepared ... so the truly reckless thing would be to do the exact opposite. I can't wait to see the look on Hugo's face when we show up with only our instincts to protect us!"

"Great," Amber grumbled, closing the secret compartment with a loud sigh. "Wait, where are we even going? Where *is* Hugo?"

"Hugo and his mother used to live in a charming little cottage in the country," Ego explained. "But then 'Mummy' decided it would be better for Hugo's career if he lived somewhere more evil."

"Like your secret island lair that we blew to smithereens?" Amber asked.

"Evil-er," Ego hissed.

Amber peered down through the clouds. Below them, surrounded by sea, was a densely forested island with a mountain rising up from its centre. A hollow mountain.

"Secret *volcano* lair!" Amber cried excitedly. "I always wanted to fight a villain with their own volcano!"

"The perfect place to face my arch-enemy," said Spynosaur, lost in a reverie.

"For the last time!" Ego howled. "I'm your arch-enemy!"

21.
AT HOME WITH THE EGOS

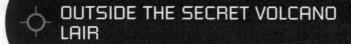

OUTSIDE THE SECRET VOLCANO LAIR

Spynosaur landed the jet near the trees at the base of the volcano. Much to his disappointment, no one had tried to shoot them down or blow them up or make any attempt on their life whatsoever. Having disembarked without incident, Spynosaur, Amber and Ergo Ego peered up at the volcano. No sooner had Spynosaur suggested they create an entrance with high explosives than a section of the volcano's base slid slowly open.

"Secret volcano lair has a secret door!" Amber

said excitedly. She hurried inside, with Spynosaur and Ergo Ego close behind. They emerged into a vast, cavernous space, fifty metres across, with several small corridors leading to chambers and anterooms. The room stretched high into the air and was covered from floor to wall with curved steel panels, riveted to the rock and polished to an impressive sheen. Dotted about the floor and ceiling were hundreds of circular vents, whose fans emitted a sinister hum as they spun and whirred.

"This place must have cost a fortune!" grumbled Ergo Ego.

"Only the best for the world's most diabolical criminal mastermind," said a voice. From one of the corridors emerged a tall woman dressed in a duck-egg blue tracksuit. She had a mountain of golden-blonde hair piled on her head, long, false nails and a tiny handbag encrusted with so many shiny jewels it was hard to look at.

"For the last time, I am the world's most diabolical— Oh, never mind!" Ego snapped.

"I thought they put you in the Bin, Ergo – where you belong," the woman said with a sneer.

"Don't start on me, Lou-Lou!" Ego snapped. "Your son's been stealing my evil plans again! Where is he?"

"Our son can't help being more villainous than you ever were," replied Lou-Lou, sidling up to Spynosaur. She took a bright red lipstick out of her handbag and spread it over her lips. "Ergo's told me all about you, Mr Spynosaur," she cooed. "He seems to think he's your arch-enemy. I tell him he needs more realistic goals, but Ergo's been a dreamer since the day we met..."

"I'm sure Spynosaur doesn't want to hear our life story," Ego hissed.

"We got together at a crime convention!" Lou-Lou continued, replacing her lipstick in her handbag. "I used to dabble in villainy back in the day – nothing bad enough to get your attention, I'm sure! But I've always thought trying to take over the world was a young person's game. After a while it just gets a bit sad ... don't you agree, Ergo?"

"Uh, Da-ad?" Amber muttered, nudging her dad's shin with her foot. "The mission...?"

"Yes, enough tripping down memory lane!" Ego snapped. "Where's Hugo?"

"Right behind you," Lou-Lou replied, pointing over Ergo Ego's shoulder.

Spynosaur turned, ready to do battle with his new arch-enemy...

But two minutes later he was playing "dinosaurs".

22.
HUGO

"Daddy!"

From the corridor behind them emerged a small boy. He was half Amber's size, with short, podgy arms and legs and a bald, egg-shaped head. He wore orange dungarees and unlaced shoes, and cradled a cuddly green dinosaur in his arms.

"That's Hugo?" Amber said. She turned to her dad, just in time to see his heart sink. There was no way this little boy could be a criminal mastermind.

They'd been tricked.

"Daddy, I got a dinosaur!" Hugo said, holding up his toy. Then he turned to Spynosaur. "You've got a dinosaur, too!"

"No, Hugo, this is Spynosaur – who, yes, happens to be a dinosaur," Ego explained, narrowing his eyes. "But you know that, because you've been stealing Daddy's evil plans again, haven't you?"

"Enough!" Spynosaur growled. He bared a mouthful of sharp teeth, his toe claws clacking against the floor. "I won't let you blame your evil schemes on an innocent boy, Ego..."

"Innocent? Ha!" scoffed Ergo Ego. "I'm telling you, my boy is bad to the bone!"

"But he's a child!" Spynosaur cried. "He's four years old!"

"Four and a half," Hugo's mother said, dabbing yet more lipstick round her mouth. "How old will you be next year, Hugo?"

"...Six?" Hugo said.

"No, you'll be five, won't you, my little bean?" said Lou-Lou. "He's not very good at counting, bless him..."

Spynosaur exhaled deeply.

"Well played, Ego," he snarled. "This whole elaborate plot was a way to ensure your freedom. You turned Department 6 against me because you knew I'd come after you. You spun a yarn about your son so I'd break you out of the Bin and bring you to your new evil lair. Well, come on then! Whatever diabolical fate you've planned for me, I'll—"

"My dinosaur looks like you!" Hugo interrupted, holding his cuddly toy up to Spynosaur, not in the least intimidated by the sight of a very real *deinonychus*. "I like trains and cars and teddies and robots but I like dinosaurs the best," he added happily. "Do you want to play?"

A smile spread across Spynosaur's face. He held up his hands and hooked his fingers to show off his claws.

"Roar," he said.

"You're a dinosaur!" giggled Hugo. "Roar! Roar!"

"Dad...?" Amber said, feeling more than a bit out of her depth.

"It's all right, Amber, he's just a little boy," Spynosaur said. He knelt down and patted Hugo's head with a scaly hand. "So, what's your dinosaur's name, Hugo?"

"He's not a dinosaur," Hugo replied, holding his toy in front of Spynosaur's face. "Look!"

Spynosaur looked down. His eyes grew wide.

The dinosaur was gone. Suddenly, Hugo was holding a real, live dog.

"It can't be..." Spynosaur muttered as the pug stared back at him, snot bubbles popping out of its nostrils. "Pugsy Malone?"

Hugo smiled. A strange, curved smile.

"May you get *everything* that is coming to you," he said. "Now, Mummy!"

Spynosaur didn't even see Lou-Lou point her lipstick at him. He just heard the FSSS! as a dart flew out from its tip and then the sharp THUP! as it lodged in his neck. He heard Amber cry "Dad!" as he crumpled to the floor...

Then everything went black.

23.
HUGO'S
DIABOLICAL PLAN

HUGO EGO'S SECRET
VOLCANO LAIR

Spynosaur woke up to find himself tied to a space rocket.

"Diabolical..." he groaned. He was suspended ten metres in the air, lashed to the towering silver rocket by thick ropes.

Spynosaur strained against the ropes but the drugged lipstick dart had left his muscles feeling like jelly. As he looked around he realized that a whole side of Hugo's lair had opened up to reveal a vast chamber containing the rocket. High above him, moonlight flooded in through an opening in the volcano's mouth.

YAP! YAP!

Spynosaur looked down to the bottom of the rocket, to see Pugsy Malone barking breathlessly back at him, cradled in the arms of Hugo Ego.

"Excellent, you're awake," squeaked Hugo, stroking Pugsy's head as he stared up at Spynosaur. "I wouldn't want you to miss the main event — especially since you're it!" he added, sounding altogether more articulate and less child-like than before.

"Hugo! Where's Amber?" Spynosaur snarled, struggling against his bonds.

"I sent her away with Mummy and Daddy," Hugo replied. "I wanted to talk to you all on my own, arch-enemy to arch-enemy."

"You can't have done all this," Spynosaur growled. "It isn't possible..."

"You mean, because I'm four and a half?" replied Hugo. "I'm an evil genius with a burning desire to take over the world – I don't have time to be four and a half."

"Then it was you in disguise as the princess's servant in the Canadian royal palace?" Spynosaur asked. "It was you who framed me?"

"Framed you, fooled you, beat you," Hugo replied, stroking Pugsy's fleshy head. "Getting the job as the princess's servant was easy – all it took was a fake beard, a pair of glasses and six interviews … but I spent nearly all my pocket money hiring a hundred thugs for that dog-napping. It was the only way to make sure I could carry out an effective test of my brain fog."

"Ah yes, brain fog – another idea stolen from your father," Spynosaur scoffed. "Do you have any original ideas, Hugo?"

"I didn't steal! My brain fog is a million times better than Daddy's!" Hugo howled, suddenly sounding like a four-year-old again. He gave Pugsy another stroke and regained his composure. "Brain fog two-point-oh is an invisible, undetectable gas comprising trillions of tiny nano-bots under my mental control. All it took was a single canister, hidden under my beard, to make everyone think they'd seen you eat poor Pugsy Malone. In all the confusion, I slipped away with this horrid hound and the rest is victory!"

"I admit, I've been *dogged* by problems ever since," Spynosaur said. "But why, Hugo? Why frame me?"

"One year ago today, my daddy tied you to a space rocket and fired you into the moon ... but then you came back as a dinosaur," Hugo explained. "Well, I decided to finish the job Daddy started. I'm going to do what Daddy could never do – I'm going to fire you into the moon *for good* and take my daddy's place as the world's most diabolical criminal mastermind!"

"The rocket to the moon thing again?" tutted Spynosaur, glancing up at the space rocket. "Still copying Daddy..."

"I didn't copy! Shut up!" Hugo snapped. He stroked a wheezing Pugsy Malone and took a deep breath to compose himself. "You think my daddy was evil? I'm about to turn the villainy up to eleven."

24.
BRAIN FOG 2.0
(AKA TURNING THE VILLAINY UP TO ELEVEN)

"Mummy! Daddy! Come and see!" called Hugo, putting Pugsy Malone on the floor. "I'm doing my diabolical plan!"

Spynosaur ground his sharp teeth as he saw Hugo's mother leading Amber out of a nearby corridor into the lair, her dart-firing lipstick pressed into Amber's back.

"Dad!" Amber cried.

"Don't worry, Amber — everything's going to be all right," Spynosaur said, but Amber wasn't sure he meant it.

"Spynosaur tied to a space rocket? That's my idea!" Ergo Ego said, emerging into the lair behind Lou-Lou and Amber. "For the last time, Hugo, stop stealing my evil plans!"

"Put a sock in it, Ergo — Hugo's already twice the villain you'll ever be," sneered Lou-Lou. "I'm so proud of my little baddie!"

"You are such an irresponsible parent," Ego hissed, glowering at Lou-Lou. "And I say that as a man who has blown up the Eiffel Tower twice."

"Shut up, Daddy, I'm talking!" Hugo Ego yelled. "I bet you stupid heads didn't even realize that my brain fog is being pumped through this lair's many vents ... which means I can make you see whatever I want!"

"I think I've seen enough for one day," Spynosaur replied. "Let's get to the business of my defeating you and clearing my—"

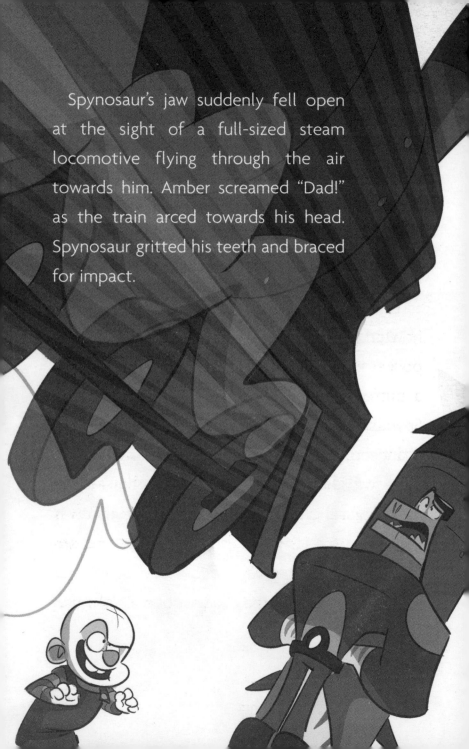

Spynosaur's jaw suddenly fell open at the sight of a full-sized steam locomotive flying through the air towards him. Amber screamed "Dad!" as the train arced towards his head. Spynosaur gritted his teeth and braced for impact.

"See?" giggled Hugo. Spynosaur looked up to find the locomotive had vanished as soon as it had appeared.

"I admit it, that got me *steamed* up," Spynosaur said with a grimace.

"It's just a stupid magic trick!" snapped a defiant Amber. "And magic tricks are for babies..."

"I'm not a baby! I'm one hundred per cent evil!" howled Hugo. He produced a control pad from a pocket in his dungarees, his finger hovering over a button marked "LAUNCH". "Here's the twist, Spynosaur! I'm going to give your sidekick the chance to save you. When I press this button, there will be exactly thirty seconds before the rocket blasts off – all your sidekick has to do is get across the lair and untie you before you are blasted to your doom!"

"Easy!" Amber roared. "I can do it, Dad! I can save you!"

"Don't be so sure, sidekick," hissed Hugo, rounding on Amber. "This room is filled with brain fog, which means I decide what you see! Can you reach Spynosaur in time, or will he be blasted into space, leaving you all alone and crying like a big crybaby?"

"OK, that's just mean," Ego said, shaking his head.

"That's my evil little sprout!" Lou-Lou laughed, clapping her hands.

"There's just one thing you didn't count on, Hugo," Spynosaur said. "Amber won't be alone ... because Jet Setter can find anyone."

"Who?" Hugo asked. A second later, the air was filled with a deafening

25.
EVERYONE VS BRAIN FOG

Shattered steel and rock flew in every direction as a huge explosion blasted a hole in the wall of the lair. Hugo turned to see Jet Setter and a small army of Department 6 agents burst into the room.

"About time, Setter," Spynosaur said with a grin.

"Told you I'd find you, darling!" said Jet Setter, spotting Spynosaur at the far end of the lair, lashed to the rocket. "And not a moment too soon, it seems..."

"Nobody move!" howled Danger Monkey,

hobbling into the lair with a crutch in one hand and a machine gun in the other. "Anyone tries to run and I'll unfriend you! I'll troll you! I'll fill yer inbox with spam!"

"Arrest everyone! Especially if they've done something wrong," boomed M11, following her agents into the lair. She surveyed the scene in horror. "Blast it to smithereens, what is all this? Somebody, report!"

Amber took a deep breath.

"Everybody thought Dad ate Pugsy Malone but actually it was an illusion caused by brain fog and Dad thought Ergo Ego had done it but then Ergo Ego realized it was Hugo Ego who'd done it 'cause Ergo Ego has a son called Hugo Ego so then Dad broke Ergo Ego out of the Bin so we could find Hugo but then when we got here we thought he was just a normal little boy but actually he's bonkers like conkers and then Hugo's mum shot my dad with a dart and Hugo tied Dad to a space rocket to finish the job his dad started and then you arrived and now, it's now," she said in a single breath. "Did I miss anything, Dad?"

"I think that about covers it," replied Spynosaur.

"Shut up shut up shut up! This doesn't change anything, you stupid heads!" screeched Hugo, holding his control pad aloft. "There's enough brain fog to go around! Goodbye, Spynosaur!"

With that, he pressed the launch button.
Amber scanned the room in a split second.

Twenty-eight seconds. I can do this," Amber muttered to herself. "Trust my instincts..."

"**STAY BACK, AMBER!**" yelled Spynosaur as the invisible brain fog flooded the room through a hundred vents. "It's too dangerous!"

But Amber did not stay back. She leaped into action ... and raced into the path of a ten-foot-tall teddy bear.

The brain fog had taken effect. They were at the mercy of Hugo Ego's illusions.

A second later, Amber had no idea where her father was — and was fighting for her life against things that didn't even exist.

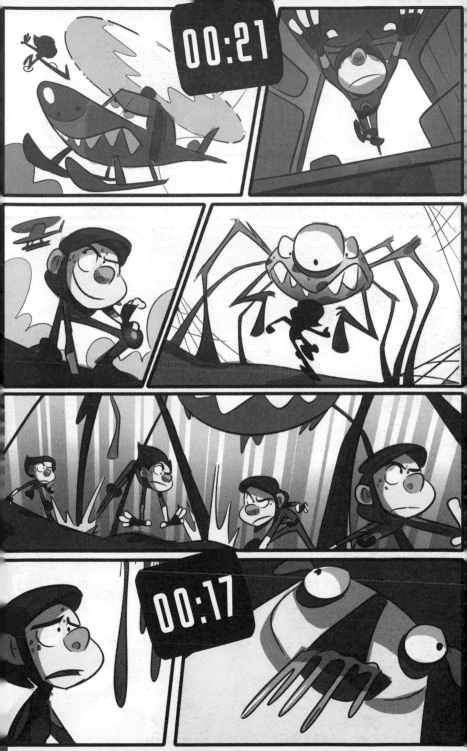

Trust my
instincts...

26.
ROCKET
TO THE MOON

Amber reached out, her eyes pressed shut. She felt sharp teeth, a scaly snout, a long bony jaw. Then, behind the noise and confusion of the brain fog, she heard her father's voice.

"Amber?"

It took Amber nine-tenths of a second to realize that she'd done it — she had managed to cross the lair to the rocket and climb the ladder to reach her father. But despite the illusions swirling around her, she could feel the blazing heat of burning fuel…

The rocket was blasting off.

"Dad!" she yelled, and wrapped her arms round her dad's neck.

"Amber, get out of here!" her dad shouted, but it was too late. Fire burst beneath them as the rocket soared upwards.

Amber clung on with all her might.

"DAAAaaaAAD!" Amber screamed. As they escaped the layer of brain fog, Amber's thoughts suddenly cleared. She opened her eyes to see the rocket zoom out of the volcano and into the night sky. Within moments Hugo's lair was far below them.

"HANG ON, AMBER!" her father roared over the din of the engines. But Amber's grip was no match for the force of the rocket's ascent. In no time, she felt her arms slipping from Spynosaur's neck…

Spynosaur's mighty jaws clamped round the collar of Amber's shirt, leaving her dangling in the air as the rocket sped ever upwards. Battling the force of the speeding rocket, Amber reached into the pocket of her trousers ... and took out a laser pen.

"LSSR PN?" Spynosaur grunted. "RR SSD NN GDJTTS!"

"WHAT?" Amber yelled over the rocket's din.

"RR SSD NN GDJTS!" her dad repeated.

"I KNOW YOU SAID NO GADGETS! BUT I THOUGHT WE COULD DO WITH— ACTUALLY, COULD WE MAYBE TALK ABOUT THIS WHEN WE'RE NOT BEING FIRED INTO THE MOON?" Amber yelled. She clicked the pen's top and a needle-thin laser beam shot out and began burning through the ropes tethering her dad to the rocket. A second later, the ropes split apart and both agents found themselves plummeting to the ground.

"AAAaaaAAH!" Amber screamed as they fell.

Above them, the rocket soared away on its journey to the moon and, below them, Hugo's secret volcano lair was coming up fast.

"Rtvvt prr-rrsshss!" Spynosaur growled.

"What?" Amber asked.

Spynosaur opened his jaws and dropped Amber into his clawed hands.

"I said, activate para-shoes!" he cried. In an instant, parachutes expanded from the soles of Spynosaur's feet and he and Amber floated head first towards the ground.

"You took the para-shoes from the jet? You said no gadgets!" Amber blurted. "What happened to 'trust your instincts'?"

"What can I say? My instincts told me to take the para-shoes," her father replied with a wink. He hugged Amber closer. "Thanks for the rescue. I was not looking forward to moon-trip number two..."

"You're welcome," Amber replied. "But you can put 'hitching a ride on a space rocket' on my list of things I do not need to do again."

The spies peered down through the volcano

to the mayhem below. Jet Setter, Danger Monkey and the other agents were still under the brain fog's influence, frantically battling invisible enemies. Hugo and his parents, meanwhile, stood at the edge of the room, looking on.

"Hugo's the key," Spynosaur said as they floated towards the volcano. "He said he controls the brain fog's effects with his mind. If we take him out, it should *deactivate* the fog and bring everyone back to their senses..."

"Then do me a favour," Amber replied. "*Drop me.*"

27.
THE BEST FOILED PLANS

Far below in the lair, Hugo Ego was enjoying every moment of his apparent victory.

"I'm the most diabolical criminal mastermind ever!" he giggled, watching M11 and the other agents battle phantom assailants, as the sound of the rocket faded to nothing.

"Yes, yes, very impressive," tutted Ergo Ego huffily. "Could I please go back to prison now?"

"Can't you just enjoy quality time with your family?" Lou-Lou tutted. "Thanks to our son,

Spynosaur is no more!"

"Actually, rumours of my rocketed-to-the-moon-ness have been greatly exaggerated," said a voice. Hugo and his parents looked up.

Spynosaur was floating head first towards them on his para-shoes, with Amber clutched in his arms.

"Now, Dad!" Amber cried. Spynosaur let go of his sidekick, and Amber dived towards Hugo Ego.

"PLAYGROUND FAIRGROUND TOUGH STUFF NO-NONSENSE NINJA-KICK!"

As it turned out, it wasn't quite a "ninja-kick" — the falling Amber just landed on top of Hugo — but it was more than enough to knock him to the floor.

"Hugo!" screamed Lou-Lou. She whipped her dart-firing lipstick out of her handbag and took aim at Amber. "You'll pay for that, you naughty girl!" she screeched. "Nobody squashes my little potato and gets away with—"

FLOMP

Spynosaur landed head first on top of Hugo's mum, knocking off Lou-Lou's aim as the dart flew from the lipstick. It streaked with a FSSSSSS! past Amber's head, missing her by a hair ... and landing with a THUP in Hugo's right buttock.

"Mummy...?" was all Hugo could muster before he drifted into unconsciousness.

"Ha! Take that, stupid head!" Ergo Ego laughed. "I mean, oh no, poor Hugo..."

"My ... little ... cabbage!" wheezed a flattened Lou-Lou. "What ... have I ... done?"

"I'd say that's *stunning* work," said Spynosaur with a smirk.

"Da-ad," Amber groaned. She rolled her eyes, but it didn't stop a great big smile spreading across her face.

20.
AFTER THE FOG
(AKA RECKLESSLY REBELLIOUS RULE-BREAKING... AND RETIREMENT)

With Hugo unconscious, the effects of his brain fog immediately subsided, leaving M11 and her agents desperately defending themselves against nothing at all. While Spynosaur and Amber tried to explain what had transpired, Ergo Ego and Lou-Lou cradled the sleeping Hugo in their arms.

"My poor little turnip! Mummy didn't mean to shoot you!" she wailed.

"This has not been the Ego family's finest hour," Ergo Ego sighed to himself. Then he reached into a pocket in his jumpsuit and took hold of the pistol Spynosaur had handed him back in the Bin. A grin spread across his face. "But the day is not over yet…"

Nearby, Danger Monkey was having a hard time separating reality from illusion.

"I could've sworn that I was just in mortal conflict with a giant toy truck!" he declared, scratching his head and bottom at the same time. "Come back 'ere, giant toy truck! I'll flatten yer tyres! I'll crack yer windscreen! I'll stick a banana up your exhaust!"

"Relax, Danger Monkey," said Spynosaur. "You should take a leaf out of my sidekick's book and trust your instincts – I wouldn't be standing here if she hadn't."

"Da-ad," groaned Amber, swelling with pride despite her embarrassment.

"Well, this lair is *teeming* with brain-fog

canisters," said Jet Setter, emerging from beneath one of the floor vents. "I've deactivated the pumps, but we should probably—"

"Blow the whole place to smithereens for good measure? Good thinking, Setter," interrupted Spynosaur. He looked down and saw Pugsy Malone wheezing at his feet.

"It appears I may owe you an apology, Spynosaur," M11 said, her moustache twitching uneasily as Spynosaur scooped Pugsy into his clawed hand. "Revoking your Right to Spy and ordering your imprisonment might have been a *slight* overreaction."

"Think nothing of it, M11," Spynosaur replied, while Pugsy licked his chin. "I suggest we put this whole thing—"

"Behind you!" shouted Amber. Everyone spun round to see Ergo Ego, aiming his pistol directly at Spynosaur's chest.

"You have handed me my victory, you stupid head!" said Ego, the pistol shaking in his hand. "I can finally rid the world of Spynosaur and prove that I am the world's most diabolical criminal master— Oh, what's the point?"

Ego threw Spynosaur's pistol to the ground.

"Ergo, you pathetic excuse for a wrongdoer!" Lou-Lou shrieked, still cradling the sleeping Hugo. "What do you think you're doing?"

"I think ... I'm *retiring*," Ego said.

"What?" Amber blurted.

Ego let out a slow, long sigh and stared at Pugsy Malone, held in Spynosaur's arms.

"Look at this dog, Spynosaur," he said.

Spynosaur peered down at Pugsy Malone, with its ridiculously squashed face and bulging eyes. "I'd rather not," he admitted.

"People bred this dog to look like it has been hit in the face with an ironing board," Ego continued. "This poor, doomed creature had its choices made for it ... but I choose to make my own. I can choose to be your enemy – and condemn my son to the same fate – or I can choose to retire from villainy and focus on family life ... from prison."

"In that case, it's been a pleasure working with you – and against you," said Spynosaur as Danger Monkey slapped Ego in cuffs. "A good arch-enemy is hard to find."

"You — you mean it?" Ego blurted. He beamed from ear to ear as Danger Monkey led him away. "Did you hear that?" added Ego. "He called me his arch-enemy…"

29.
INSTINCTS

An hour later, M11 and the other agents were heading back to headquarters with the captured Egos. It was safe to say no one was sure what to do with a four-and-a-half-year-old criminal mastermind, but Ergo Ego did his best to assure everyone he could teach Hugo to make his mark on the world without being villainous.

Spynosaur and Amber stayed behind, planting enough explosives in Hugo's lair to blow it to smithereens three times over. After the last

explosive was set, they took off in their jet and circled the lair. Amber's fingers itched at the thought of activating the remote detonator switch.

"Dad?" she said. "Did you know Ergo Ego still had that pistol?"

"My instincts told me that Ego would do the right thing in the end," her dad replied cryptically. "Just like your instincts told you that you could save your old dad."

"I s'pose," Amber said. "I do miss the days when we actually had a plan, though."

"Well, *not* having a plan certainly added a little excitement to the mission ... but you might have a point," Spynosaur concluded. "After all, if it wasn't for you, my plan not to have a plan would not have been the best plan I'd planned not to plan at all."

"Huh?" Amber replied.

Spynosaur switched the jet to autopilot. He turned to Amber and placed his clawed hands on her shoulders.

"Amber, one year ago today Ergo Ego tied me to a space rocket and fired me into the moon. Spyence gave me another chance at life. But today, it was *you* who saved me ... saved me *and* the day," Spynosaur said. "You're turning into quite the spy. One day, you'll be an even better agent than me."

"You – you really think so?" Amber replied, taken aback.

Her dad smiled and gave her a hug. "I know so," he replied, squeezing her tightly. "One day, Amber, you will be the world's greatest secret agent."

Amber squeezed her dad back. In that moment, she felt like she could take on every criminal mastermind at once ... she felt like she could take on the world.

"World's greatest..." she said. She looked over her dad's shoulder to the detonator switch and a grin spread across her face. "Sooo, you're saying I should trust my instincts, right?"

"That's more or less *all* I've said for the last two days," said Spynosaur. "Why do you ask?"

"'Cause my instincts are telling me to do this," Amber replied – and flicked the switch.

HE'S THE SPY THAT SURPRISES!
HE'S THE AGENT WHO'LL AMAZE!

FIGHTING FOR RIGHT, THANKS TO THOSE
SUPER-SCIENCE RAYS

THEY SAID HE ATE A DOG,
BUT THAT WASN'T EVEN TRUE,

NOW HE'S BACK TO SAVING ME,
AND HE'S BACK TO SAVING YOU!

SPYNOSAUR!

SO IF YOU NEED A HERO WHO'S A
CUT ABOVE THE REST

THEN DO WHAT HUGO EGO DID AND
PUT HIM TO THE TEST

AMBER AND HER FATHER ARE
ON HAND TO SAVE THE DAY

AND BLOW STUFF UP TO SMITHEREENS
IF IT GETS IN THEIR WAY!

SPYNOSAUR!

SPYNOSAUUUUUR!

Want to know the secrets of
DEPARTMENT 6?

Discover more

SPYNOSAUR
MISSIONS!

SPYNOSAUR

SPYNOSAUR VS GOLDENCLAW

SPYNOSAUR IN THE SPY'S THE LIMIT